Andrea
Crabtree

Pteranodon
ter-AN-a-don

Montanaceratops
mon-TAN-a-ser-a-tops

Allosaurus
AL-a-saw-russ

Stegoceras
steg-OSS-air-uss

Diplodocus
dih-PLOD-a-kuss

Mussaurus
moo-SAW-russ

Syntarsus
sin-TAR-suss

Oviraptor
o-vee-RAP-tor

Compsognathus
komp-so-NAY-thuss

Ceratosaurus
ser-AT-a-saw-russ

Segisaurus
SEE-gih-saw-russ

Monoclonius
mon-a-KLO-nee-uss

Microceratops
mike-row-SER-a-tops

Corythosaurus
ko-RITH-a-saw-russ

Pachyrhinosaurus
PAK-ee-rye-no-saw-russ

Triceratops
try-SER-a-tops

Micropachycephalosaurus
mike-row-pak-ee-SEF-a-la-saw-russ

Teratosaurus
ter-AT-a-saw-russ

Saltopus
SALT-o-pus

Dilophosaurus
dye-LO-fa-saw-russ

Camarasaurus
KAM-a-ra-saw-russ

Protoceratops
pro-toe-SER-a-tops

Scutellosaurus
scoo-TELL-o-saw-russ

Spinosaurus
SPY-na-saw-russ

Psittacosaurus
SIT-a-ka-saw-russ

Ouranosaurus
our-AN-a-saw-russ

A
Dinosaur
Named
after Me

by Bernard Most

A Voyager Book
Harcourt Brace & Company
SAN DIEGO   NEW YORK   LONDON

Requests for permission to make copies of any part of the work should be mailed to:
Permissions Department, Harcourt Brace & Company,
6277 Sea Harbor Drive, Orlando, Florida 32887-6777.

The author wishes to acknowledge the following books as sources for the factual information contained in the text:
A Field Guide to Dinosaurs by David Lambert
The Illustrated Dinosaur Dictionary by Helen Roney Sattler
Dinosaur Dictionary by Donald F. Glut

Library of Congress Cataloging-in-Publication Data
Most, Bernard.
   A dinosaur named after me/by Bernard Most.—1st ed.
      p.   cm.
   Summary: Draws parallels between the physical characteristics and capabilities of particular dinosaurs and specific children and incorporates the name of each child into that of the dinosaur.
   ISBN 0-15-223494-2
   ISBN 0-15-223493-4 (pbk.)
   1. Dinosaurs—Juvenile literature. [1. Dinosaurs.] I. Title.
QE862.D5M693   1991
567.9'1—dc20   90-36272

A B C D E
A B C D E (pbk.)

Printed in Singapore

The illustrations in this book were done in Pantone markers on Bainbridge board 172, hot press finish.
Composition by Typelink, Inc., San Diego, California
Color separations were made by Bright Arts, Ltd., Singapore.
Printed and bound by Tien Wah Press, Singapore
This book was printed on Leykam recycled paper, which contains more than 20 percent postconsumer waste and has a total recycled content of at least 50 percent.
Production supervision by Warren Wallerstein and Ginger Boyer
Designed by Alex P. Mendoza

To Harcourt Brace's
very own DIANE-osaur,
my editor, Diane D'Andrade

Apatosaurus (ah-PAT-a-saw-russ)

My favorite dinosaur is Apatosaurus.
This is the correct scientific name
for Brontosaurus, which was
thought to be a new dinosaur
when it was discovered.
But scientists now think it
is the same as a dinosaur
discovered years earlier,
Apatosaurus. I like the name
A-PAT-osaurus much
better anyway.

Pat

Brontosaurus (BRON-ta-saw-russ)

Ron

My favorite dinosaur is Brontosaurus. Everyone knows this dinosaur as Brontosaurus—so why change it? Many scientists today think dinosaurs were more like mammals and birds than reptiles. But no one wants to change the name *dinosaur,* which means "terrible lizard." If you must change the name of Brontosaurus, call it RON-tosaurus!

Pentaceratops (PEN-ta-ser-a-tops)

My favorite dinosaur was Triceratops . . .
until I read about Pentaceratops. Its name
means "five-horned face" because it had
two more horns than Triceratops. It also
had a much larger frill. Since I was
born on the fifth day of the fifth month,
five is my lucky number. This
dinosaur should be named
BEN-taceratops!

Ben

Anodontosaurus (an-a-dont-a-SAW-russ)

My favorite dinosaur is Anodontosaurus. This armored dinosaur's name means "toothless lizard" because its jaw was discovered without any teeth. I was reading about this dinosaur with my grandma. Because I'm losing my baby teeth, she said she would call this dinosaur ANDREW-dontosaurus.

Andrew

Iguanodon (ig-WAN-a-don)

My favorite dinosaur is Iguanodon.
This plant eater is always pictured with its
big spiky thumbs pointed up.
Scientists think it used its spiky thumbs
to defend against meat eaters.
Nobody does a better imitation of
one than I do. Would you dare
to shake hands with
Iguano-DAN?

Dan

Yaleosaurus (YALE-ee-a-saw-russ)

My favorite dinosaur is Yaleosaurus. It was named after Yale University because its fossils were found near the school. Yale's museum has a great dinosaur collection. When I grow up, I want to be a student at Yale and learn so much about this dinosaur they will rename it GAIL-eosaurus!

Gail

Aristosuchus (a-RISS-ta-sook-uss)

My favorite dinosaur is Aristosuchus.
Scientists first thought this meat eater's fossils were
from a crocodile, so they named
it "best crocodile." I love
reading about crocodiles
and dinosaurs. But if I
discover a dinosaur
that reminds me of a
crocodile, I will name it
CHRIS-tosuchus!

Chris

Brachiosaurus (BRAK-ee-a-saw-russ)

My favorite dinosaur is Brachiosaurus.
It was a member of the tallest
dinosaur family and could reach
higher than any other dinosaur.
I am the tallest person in
my class, and I can reach
higher than anybody.
I would have named
Brachiosaurus after me:
ZACH-iosaurus.

Zach

Lambeosaurus (LAM-bay-a-saw-russ)

My favorite dinosaur is Lambeosaurus. Scientists think it made loud, trumpet-like sounds with its hollow crest. When I play my trumpet, I close my eyes and wonder if I sound anything like this dinosaur. Was I surprised to find out its other scientific name is STEPHAN-osaurus!

Stephan

Ankylosaurus (an-KILE-a-saw-russ)

My favorite dinosaur is Ankylosaurus.
Rows of bony plates and a clublike tail
protected this peaceful plant eater from meat
eaters. Every time I visit the museum and
see a knight's armor, I think about
this largest armored dinosaur. But
a much better name would be
HANK-ylosaurus!

Hank

Microvenator (mike-row-ven-AY-tor)

My favorite dinosaur is Microvenator, or "small hunter." This turkey-sized meat eater was good at catching its dinner because it was very fast and had grasping claws. I'm a small hunter, too. I'm good at catching my friends when we play hide-and-seek. "Ready or not, here comes MIKE-rovenator!"

Mike

Maiasaura (my-a-SAW-ra)

My favorite dinosaur is Maiasaura.
Named "good mother lizard" because it was
found near a nest with fifteen baby
dinosaurs, scientists think it brought
food to its babies and took good
care of them. Mom says I take good
care of my baby brother. She says
this dinosaur's name should be
MARY-asaura.

Mary

Stegosaurus (STEG-a-saw-russ)

My favorite dinosaur is Stegosaurus.
Scientists think the large plates that covered
its back were for protection and made
Stegosaurus look larger to meat-eating
dinosaurs—just like my shoulder
pads protect me and make me look
larger to opposing teams.
My friends renamed Stegosaurus
GREG-osaurus.

Greg

Dravidosaurus (dra-VID-a-saw-russ)

David

My favorite dinosaur is Dravidosaurus. It was a member of the Stegosaurus family but one of the littlest, only ten feet long. It's like a little brother to Stegosaurus. I'm Greg's little brother, so if they change Stegosaurus to GREG-osaurus, I hope they change Dravidosaurus to DAVID-osaurus!

Avimimus (a-vee-MY-muss)

My favorite dinosaur is Avimimus.
There was much that was birdlike
about this little insect eater with
feathered wings. Some scientists
think modern birds evolved
from dinosaurs. I would like
to help prove that birds are
living dinosaurs so they
could rename this dinosaur
AMY-mimus.

Amy

Tyrannosaurus Rex (tie-RAN-a-saw-russ REX)

My favorite dinosaur is Tyrannosaurus Rex,
the biggest, meanest, fiercest,
most powerful meat eater ever found.
It had teeth like giant knives.
Scientists named it "king of
the tyrant lizards."
Sometimes, when I have
a bad day or lose my temper,
my dad calls me
RYAN-osaurus Rex!

Ryan

Macrurosaurus (mak-ROO-ra-saw-russ)

My favorite dinosaur is Macrurosaurus, named "long-tailed lizard" because all they found of it were forty tailbones miles apart. They think this long tail belonged to a four-legged plant eater. That gave me an idea for a dinosaur game. I call it "Pin the tail on MARK-rurosaurus."

Mark

Kentrosaurus (KEN-tra-saw-russ)

My favorite dinosaur is KEN-trosaurus.
This "pointed lizard" had spikes
running from the top of its head
to the tip of its tail. That's why
I love drawing this dinosaur.
My friend Glenn says it would
be his favorite if it were
renamed GLENN-trosaurus.
But I like its name just the way it is.

Ken

Ornithomimus (orn-ith-a-MY-muss)

My favorite dinosaur is Ornithomimus. It belonged to the "ostrich dinosaur" family, the fastest dinosaurs. Scientists think they ran even faster than modern racehorses. I'm so fast, someday I'm going to win a gold medal in the Olympics. Then they could name the fastest dinosaur ANN-ithomimus.

Ann

Ammosaurus (AM-a-saw-russ)

My favorite dinosaur is Ammosaurus.
Its name means "sand lizard" because
of where its fossils were found. My
brother calls me sand lizard
because I like to play in the
sand so much. He says they should
change this dinosaur's name
from Ammosaurus to
SAM-osaurus.

Sam

Pterodactylus (ter-a-DAK-tie-luss)

My favorite is not a dinosaur.
It's Pterodactylus, a flying cousin of dinosaurs.
Some pterodactyls were tiny, like sparrows.
Others were much bigger, like hawks.
Scientists think they caught
insects in the air. I made my own
Pterodactylus kite. It's a
TERRY-dactylus!

Terry

Parasaurolophus (par-a-saw-ROL-a-fuss)

My favorite dinosaur is Parasaurolophus.
What made this duckbilled dinosaur different
was a long, hollow tube on top of its head.
Its use remains a mystery. Scientists
at first thought it was used as a snorkel,
but it was closed at the top. Still,
when I go snorkeling I pretend I am
GARY-saurolophus.

Gary

Nanosaurus (NAN-a-saw-russ)

My favorite dinosaur is Nanosaurus, which means "dwarf lizard," because it was so little, just like my cat. It was very light on its feet, just like my cat, and it was very speedy, just like my cat. If I had discovered this lively little dinosaur, I would have named it after my cat, IVAN-osaurus.

Ivan

Plateosaurus (PLAY-tee-a-saw-russ)

My favorite dinosaur is Plateosaurus.
This dinosaur's name means "flat lizard"
because it had flat, platelike teeth for
chewing leaves. Although it sometimes
ate meat, it was a vegetarian most
of the time, just like me!
I even love to plant my own
vegetables. So it's only natural
to call this dinosaur
KATY-osaurus!

Katy

Erlikosaurus (er-LIK-a-saw-russ)

My favorite dinosaur is Erlikosaurus. It was unusual because of its toothless beak, sharp teeth on the sides of its jaws, and webbed toes. Scientists think it was an expert fish catcher. My dad is teaching me how to fish. I'm going to be the best fish catcher ever. Then they could call this dinosaur ERIC-osaurus.

Eric

"Supersaurus" (SOO-per-saw-russ)

My favorite dinosaur is "Supersaurus."
All that was found were a few giant bones in Colorado,
so it doesn't have an official
name yet. It may have
been even bigger than
Brachiosaurus. I'm going on
vacation to Colorado. If I
help find the rest of its
bones, they could name it
SUE-persaurus.

Sue

Dinosaurs (DIE-na-sawrs)

I don't have a favorite dinosaur,
because they are all my favorites.
I love reading about every one of them.
If I had my way, I would change their
name from dinosaurs to
DIANE-osaurs.

Diane

Think about your favorite dinosaur.
Wouldn't you like a dinosaur named after

YOU ?

Pterodactylus
ter-a-DAK-tie-luss

Iguanodon
ig-WAN-a-don

Ornithomimus
orn-ith-a-MY-muss

Plateosaurus
PLAY-tee-a-saw-russ

Microvenator
mike-row-ven-AY-tor

Apatosaurus
ah-PAT-a-saw-russ

Brontosaurus
BRON-ta-saw-russ

Brachiosaurus
BRAK-ee-a-saw-russ

Ammosaurus
AM-a-saw-russ

Nanosaurus
NAN-a-saw-russ

Dravidosaurus
dra-VID-a-saw-russ

Yaleosaurus
YALE-ee-a-saw-russ

Anodontosaurus
an-a-dont-a-SAW-russ

Avimimus
a-vee-MY-muss

Pentaceratops
PEN-ta-ser-a-tops

Aristosuchus
a-RISS-ta-sook-uss

Kentrosaurus
KEN-tra-saw-russ

Macrurosaurus
mak-ROO-ra-saw-russ

Maiasaura
my-a-SAW-ra

Supersaurus
SOO-per-saw-russ

Tyrannosaurus Rex
tie-RAN-a-saw-russ REX

Ankylosaurus
an-KILE-a-saw-russ

Lambeosaurus
LAM-bay-a-saw-russ

Stegosaurus
STEG-a-saw-russ

Erlikosaurus
er-LIK-a-saw-russ

Parasaurolophus
par-a-saw-ROL-a-fuss